Bea & Mr. Jones

Story and pictures by

Amy Schwartz

Harcourt, Inc.

Orlando Austin New York San Diego Toronto London

Manufactured in China

www.HarcourtBooks.com

First published in 1982 by The Bradbury Press
Published 1983 by Picture Puffins, a division of Penguin Group (USA) Inc.
Published 1994 by Aladdin Books, a division of Simon & Schuster, Inc.

Library of Congress Cataloging-in-Publication Data
Schwartz, Amy.
Bea and Mr. Jones: story and pictures by Amy Schwartz.
p. cm.
Summary: Tired of kindergarten, Bea Jones trades "jobs" with her father, who works in an office.
[1. Schools—Fiction. 2. Work—Fiction.] I. Title: Bea and Mister Jones.   II. Title.
PZ7.S406Be 2006
[E]—dc22   2005029682
ISBN-13: 978-0-15-205811-1 ISBN-10: 0-15-205811-7

First Harcourt edition 2006

H G F E D C B A

Manufactured in China

The illustrations in this book were done in pencil on Rives BFK paper.
The display and text type was set in Sauna.
Color separations by Bright Arts Ltd., Hong Kong
Manufactured by South China Printing Co., Ltd., China
This book was printed on totally chlorine-free Stora Enso Matte paper.
Production supervision by Jane Van Gelder
Designed by Lauren Rille

For my parents

I've had it with kindergarten!" Bea Jones said to her father as he was sitting down to breakfast.

"I've had it with beanbag games!

"I've had it with clothespin games!

"I've had it with sitting on that dumb green rug and playing that dumb colored lollipop game!

"I'm ready for a change."

Mr. Jones put down his muffin and coffee. "Beatrice," he said, "do you think I like my job? I'm tired of running for the 7:45! I'm tired of sitting at that desk and working so hard! I'm tired of laughing at the boss's jokes all day!"

"Doesn't sound so bad to me," said Bea.

Mr. Jones looked thoughtfully at his daughter. "Beatrice," he said, "*what if* we trade places today?"

Bea smiled. "Actually," she said, "that makes perfect sense to me."

And so, after breakfast, Bea put on her father's coat and tie. She looked very important. Mr. Jones put on his sneakers and turned cartwheels for a while. He felt better immediately.

Bea caught the 7:45 with time to spare. She slid onto the empty seat next to her father's business associate and best friend, Harvey Hopkins.

"Morning, Harvey," she said, and then explained that she would be taking her father's place today.

"Well," said Harvey, "today is going to be *dreadful*.
This afternoon is the deadline for the Crumbly Crackers
campaign, and we haven't come up with a thing!"

Bea patted Harvey's hand reassuringly as the train
pulled out of the station.

The train reached the city and Bea and Harvey hurried to the Smith Building. They took the elevator to the forty-second floor and walked into Smith & Smith Advertising.

Harvey sent around a memo which read:

```
Attention: All Executives
      Please note that Mr. Jones
      will not be with us today.
      He is at kindergarten.
      Bea Jones will be taking
      his place.
```

And Bea introduced herself all around.

Meanwhile, Mr. Jones had also arrived safely
and soundly at Miss Seymour's kindergarten class.
He figured the tallest person in the class was
Miss Seymour, and handed her a note which read:

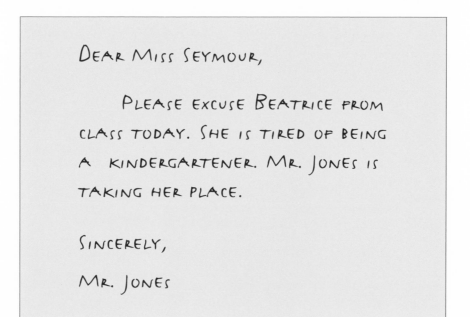

DEAR MISS SEYMOUR,

    PLEASE EXCUSE BEATRICE FROM
CLASS TODAY. SHE IS TIRED OF BEING
A KINDERGARTENER. MR. JONES IS
TAKING HER PLACE.

SINCERELY,

MR. JONES

"Well," Miss Seymour sputtered, "I must say,
this is rather unusual. But——since I do have a note
from the child's father," and she looked over her
glasses at Mr. Jones, "I suppose it must be all right
with me."

Well, Mr. Jones loved being in kindergarten.
He was a whiz at the colored lollipop game.
"Vermilion red, I believe."
Miss Seymour told him he was almost as
bright as Jimmy Davis, the class genius.

At snack time, Mr. Jones was chosen as milk and cookie monitor, and he didn't spill a thing.

At recess, he helped Miss Seymour get Jimmy Davis down
from the magnolia tree. Miss Seymour told Mr. Jones that
he was a big help.

In fact, Mr. Jones was rapidly becoming the teacher's pet.
"Oh, Mr. Jones," Miss Seymour sighed, "you're wonderful."

Back at Smith & Smith, Bea was fitting in just
fine, too. The first thing she did was give her
secretary the day off. Then she sharpened all her
pencils and drew a nice picture on her blotter.
She was very busy.

At the board meeting, Bea laughed harder than anyone at the boss's jokes. She thought they were great.

"To get to the other side?" Bea chuckled. "That's wonderful!"

Best of all, Bea came up with a wonderful new jingle
for Crumbly Crackers, just in time to save the account.
"Gentlemen, listen to this—

Munchy Crunchy my dear snackers,
You will love our Crumbly Crackers."

"Astounding!"

"A genius!"

That afternoon, Bea was offered a promotion.

When Mr. Jones came to pick up Bea at the train station, they were both very tired, but very happy.

"I feel more relaxed than I have in twenty years!" said Mr. Jones.

"I love advertising! What a challenge!" said Bea.

So, the next day Mr. Jones went to kindergarten
and Bea went to the office once again.
And the next day, and the next, and the next.
At work, Bea was made president of toy sales.

And at kindergarten, Mr. Jones continued to astound Miss Seymour and his classmates with his extraordinary intelligence.

Mr. Jones and Bea had each found their proper niche in the world.

So, remember that big kid you saw getting in for half price at the movie matinee, and you just couldn't believe he was under twelve?

Well, you were probably right.

And remember that very short executive you
saw having lunch with your father last Thursday?

Well, perhaps you know who that was, too.